SPOTLIGHT ON GEORGIA

GEORGIA DURING THE NEW SOUTH ERA

SAM CROMPTON

PowerKiDS press.

New York

Published in 2018 by The Rosen Publishing Group, Inc.
29 East 21st Street, New York, NY 10010

Editor: Melissa Raé Shofner
Book Design: Micheal Flynn
Interior Layout: Rachel Rising

Photo Credits: Cover (Felton) https://commons.wikimedia.org/wiki/File:Rebecca_L._Felton.png; Cover (Washington, Grady) pp. 7, 11, 17 Courtesy of the Library of Congress; p. 5 Horace Bradley, Harper's Weekly; pp. 5, 9, 25 (background) Reinhold Leitner/Shutterstock.com; p. 9 (Colquitt, Brown) Kean Collection/Archive Photos/Getty Images; p. 9 (Gordon) https://commons.wikimedia.org/wiki/File:Jbgordon.jpg; p. 10 Sonia Dubois/Shutterstock.com; p. 13 ullstein bild/ullstein bild/Getty Images; pp. 14, 29 Bettmann/Bettmann/Getty Images; p. 15 https://commons.wikimedia.org/wiki/File:PlessySignFront.JPG; p. 18 Library of Congress/Corbis Histroical/Getty Images; pp. 19, 21 Everett Historical/Shutterstock.com; p. 23 https://commons.wikimedia.org/wiki/File:WEB_DuBois_1918.jpg; p. 25 https://upload.wikimedia.org/wikipedia/commons/4/41/Le_Petit_Journal_7_Oct_1906.jpg; p. 27 Raymond Boyd/ Micheal Ochs Archives/Getty Images; p. 28 https://upload.wikimedia.org/wikipedia/en/6/67/Leo-frank-police-have-the-strangler-headline.jpg.

Library of Congress Cataloging-in-Publication Data

Cataloging-in-Publication Data
Names: Crompton, Sam.
Title: Georgia during the new south era / Sam Crompton.
Description: New York : PowerKids Press, 2018. | Series: Spotlight on Georgia | Includes index.
Identifiers: ISBN 9781508160014 (pbk.) | ISBN 9781508160045 (library bound) | ISBN 9781508160021 (6 pack)
Subjects: LCSH: Georgia--Juvenile literature. | Southern States--History--1865-1951--Juvenile literature.
Classification: LCC F286.3 C76 2018 | DDC 975.8--dc23

Manufactured in the United States of America

CPSIA Compliance Information: Batch #BS17PK For further information contact Rosen Publishing, New York, New York at 1-800-237-9932.

CONTENTS

CHAPTER ONE

REBUILDING AFTER RECONSTRUCTION

At the end of the era of Reconstruction, Georgia was in very poor shape. The wounds caused by the Civil War had not yet healed. Many areas of the state were still in ruins, and many Georgians still hadn't recovered. During Reconstruction, slavery was replaced with new systems of farming, such as **sharecropping**. These systems caused both black and white farmers to owe very large amounts of money.

Despite these hardships, **progressive** Georgians attempted to rebuild the state and work toward industrial growth. Many southerners were still farmers, but they began practicing new methods to make their farms more **efficient**. Many Georgians turned to the crop that had always been their strongest: cotton.

Unfortunately, **white supremacy** continued to plague black Georgians during this era. While some leaders worked to make Georgia better for white Georgians, they often neglected African Americans.

THE NEW SOUTH.

SUPPLEMENT TO HARPER'S WEEKLY, FEBRUARY 12, 1887.

THE MARKET-PLACE OF A GEORGIA VILLAGE IN THE COTTON SEASON.—Drawn by Graham and Durkin.—[See Article "The Industrial South," Page 111.]

This special "New South" section of *Harper's Weekly* from 1887 shows a busy Georgian marketplace during cotton season.

CHAPTER TWO

HENRY W. GRADY

Henry W. Grady was born in Athens, Georgia, in 1850. In the 1880s, he worked as the editor of the *Atlanta Constitution*, a Georgian newspaper. Like other **entrepreneurs** and landowners in Georgia, Grady used his position to become a booster for 19th-century Georgia. A booster is a person who promotes, or boosts, the image of a person, place, or business.

In 1886, Grady visited New York City. Standing in front of a group of businessmen, he spoke of the "New South." Grady had created the term in 1874 and his writings and speeches made it popular. He encouraged northern businessmen to move their industries south. He also spoke of the racial problems in Georgia. He believed they were mostly over. Black people were now treated well in the South, he said. This simply wasn't true.

Henry W. Grady used his power in journalism to push for the redevelopment of Georgia's economy in the 1880s. He believed Georgia had a lot to offer and used this as a selling point for his idea of a "New South."

CHAPTER THREE

THE BOURBON TRIUMVIRATE

Georgian politicians recognized the need to modernize the southern economy. Joseph E. Brown, Alfred H. Colquitt, and John B. Gordon had been important leaders for the Confederacy during the Civil War. These three men dominated Georgia politics from 1872 to 1890. They controlled two U.S. Senate positions and the office of governor. Brown, Colquitt, and Gordon held these positions for quite some time and became known as the "Bourbon Triumvirate." A triumvirate is a group of three people or things.

Brown, Colquitt, and Gordon promoted the New South ideas for commercial and industrial development in Georgia. These men were also supporters of "Lost Cause" ideals. This way of thinking attempted to maintain the nobility of Confederate beliefs after the end of the Civil War. It also downplayed the role of slavery as a cause of the Civil War. Lost Cause supporters focused more on states' rights and hostility from the North.

The Bourbon Triumvirate and other like-minded Georgians promoted an economical state government, low taxes, few services, and the use of convicts for labor at farms and factories. They also promoted white supremacy.

CHAPTER FOUR

THE POPULISTS

Toward the end of the 1880s, cotton prices fell throughout the South. Farmers were hit very hard. In response, a group called the Farmers' Alliance formed in Texas to fight for the rights of poor farmers. African Americans weren't allowed in this group, so they created the Colored Farmers' Alliance in 1886. The Georgia Farmers' Alliance formed in 1887.

These groups argued that farmers needed to break free from the hold that big businesses had on them. They also wanted bank reform and loans for farmers, among other things. When members of the Republican and Democratic parties ignored their demands, some members of these alliances formed the People's Party, also called the Populist Party.

JUTE BALING TWINE

In 1888, the price of jute baling twine, a type of string used to wrap cotton, rose sharply. The Georgia Farmer's Alliance successfully **boycotted** the manufacturers.

The Populist Party had several **vocal** and influential leaders. Thomas E. Watson was a well-known Georgian politician. Originally a liberal Democrat, Watson became a Populist and fought for the rights of poor farmers and sharecroppers.

Watson was a respected lawyer and talented speaker. He was elected to the Georgia state **legislature** in 1882, but soon decided to resign because he opposed the New South movement. He supported the traditional agricultural economy over the move to industrialization.

As a Populist leader, Watson spoke about the need to include both white and black farmers. He knew the Populist Party would need black votes. However, by the early 1900s, Watson revealed himself to be an unwavering white supremacist.

The Populist Party wasn't powerful enough to gain enough Democratic voters, and it only lasted until the early 1900s. However, it had a lasting effect on Georgia politics.

Watson returned to law, but he remained involved in Georgia politics well into the 1900s through his writings. He persuaded many white Georgians to distrust their black neighbors. This left a lasting impression on the people and politics of Georgia.

Shortly after resigning from the legislature in 1883, Watson founded the *People's Party Paper* and served as editor. This newspaper championed the ideals of the Populist Party.

CHAPTER FIVE

JIM CROW LAWS

In the decades after the Civil War, voters in the South approved new laws that prevented blacks from voting and sometimes barred them from owning property. These laws, which became known as Jim Crow laws, were designed to **disenfranchise** black people by locking them out of political and economic systems.

If black facilities and white facilities were "equal," they could remain separate. They were rarely equal, though.

In 1896, in the case of *Plessy v. Ferguson*, the Supreme Court ruled that public facilities—including trains, bathrooms, and even drinking fountains—could be kept "separate but equal" for white people and black people. There could be a fountain for white people only and a fountain for black people only. Jim Crow laws were designed to prevent African Americans from having the rights white people took for granted. The name "Jim Crow" comes from a **minstrel show** from the 1820s and 1830s. The character of that name came to represent all black people for many white people.

CHAPTER SIX

BLACK RESPONSE

African Americans knew they couldn't fight the Supreme Court ruling, at least not right away. Many blacks knew they had to fight this battle themselves since white politicians refused to help them. Two people who did this extremely well were John and Lugenia Burns Hope.

John Hope was a native Georgian who married Lugenia Burns in 1897 in Chicago. In 1898, they moved to Atlanta, where Hope taught at Atlanta Baptist Seminary, which became Morehouse College. He later became the college's first black president.

Burns Hope became a social **activist** and community organizer. For 25 years, she led the Neighborhood Union, a group designed to help black women. Black men often benefited from its actions, too. Burns Hope worked tirelessly. She established day-care facilities and other programs. With Burns Hope's help, blacks in Atlanta had better opportunities than those in any other southern city.

John Hope helped bring about the financing and construction of University Homes, the first public housing project for blacks to be funded by the U.S. government. John Hope Homes, shown here, was later built by the Atlanta Housing Authority and named in honor of John Hope.

CHAPTER SEVEN

THE 1895 ATLANTA COTTON EXPOSITION

During the late 1800s, fairs and **expositions** became popular ways to draw people to cities and display new inventions. In 1895, Atlanta hosted one of the largest cotton expositions the South had ever seen. Over 100 days, about 800,000 people came to see new farm machinery and admire the success of the cotton-producing farms. This event helped attract businesses and investors to Atlanta. The planners of the 1895 exposition also hoped to increase trade between the southern states and countries in South America and Europe.

THE 1895 ATLANTA COTTON EXPOSITION

Washington was a great public speaker. He gave many speeches throughout the North and South in his lifetime.

The leaders of the 1895 cotton exposition wanted to show they supported the New South. They asked Booker T. Washington to give a speech. Washington was one of the richest and most successful African Americans of the time. For 20 years, Washington had been known as a strong supporter of industrial education for African Americans.

When Washington took the stage at the cotton exposition, he told a story about a lost ship and a rescue ship. The people in the lost ship kept asking for water. Each time, the rescue ship put up signal flags that read, "Cast down your bucket where you are." In other words, the lost ship was already in water that was safe to drink.

Washington used this opening theme to illustrate his plan for African Americans. He said black people needed to "cast down their bucket" and find work where they were. They needed to become carpenters and cleaners, street sweepers and mechanics before they could become professors and artists, businessmen and scientists. Washington's speech disappointed some and angered others because it encouraged blacks to accept social inequality. Washington believed social equality would come to them in time.

Washington was born into slavery and worked his way up to be an educator. His speech at the 1895 cotton expo came to be known as the Atlanta Compromise address.

CHAPTER EIGHT

THE SOULS OF BLACK FOLK

W. E. B. Du Bois was another African American leader of the era. His childhood and his message were quite different from Booker T. Washington's. Du Bois did not grow up in slavery. He lived in Great Barrington, Massachusetts, before he moved south to teach at Atlanta University. Du Bois did not like Washington's message at all. He expressed his own message in the book *The Souls of Black Folk*.

Du Bois argued that blacks needed to aim high and needed to do so right away. They'd already been carpenters and mechanics. It was time for them to become educated social leaders. Du Bois argued that blacks had survived slavery and sharecropping, and they needed to fight for their civil rights.

Du Bois and Washington came to dislike each other. This was unfortunate because the African American community needed both these skilled and powerful leaders.

In 1909, Du Bois cofounded the NAACP, or the National Association for the Advancement of Colored People. The NAACP works to ensure equal rights for all people and fights against racial discrimination.

CHAPTER NINE

ATLANTA RACE RIOT

Atlanta's population grew quickly in the late 1800s and early 1900s. Both blacks and whites competed for jobs. In addition, **tensions** between the races increased as white groups feared calls for equal rights and the rise of a black upper class.

The tension erupted into violence in September 1906. Atlanta experienced the worst race riot of its history. The event was sparked by newspaper reports that four white women had been sexually assaulted by black men over the course of several days. These reports, none of which were ever proven true, led to attacks on African Americans throughout the city.

On September 22, thousands of white men gathered in downtown Atlanta to protest. The group grew larger and began to attack black people and businesses. State military forces were called to Atlanta. Nearly 100 blacks and two whites were killed in the riot.

Le Petit Journal

Le Petit Journal
CHAQUE JOUR — 6 PAGES — 5 CENTIMES
Administration : 61, rue Lafayette

Le Supplément illustré
CHAQUE SEMAINE 5 CENTIMES

5 Centimes SUPPLÉMENT ILLUSTRÉ 5 Centimes

Le Petit Journal Militaire, Maritime, Colonial.... 10 cent.
Le Petit Journal agricole, 5 cent. La Mode du Petit Journal, 10 cent.
Le Petit Journal illustré de La Jeunesse.... 10 cent.
On s'abonne sans frais dans tous les bureaux de poste

ABONNEMENTS

	SIX MOIS	UN AN
SEINE ET SEINE-ET-OISE	2 fr.	3 fr. 50
DÉPARTEMENTS	2 fr.	4 fr. »
ÉTRANGER	2 50	5 fr. »

Les manuscrits ne sont pas rendus

Dix-septième année — DIMANCHE 7 OCTOBRE 1906 — Numero 829

LES « LYNCHAGES » AUX ÉTATS-UNIS
Massacre de nègres à Atlanta (Georgie)

The Atlanta riot, illustrated here, and its outcome shocked the people of Georgia and the United States. Many African Americans turned away from the message of Washington and embraced Du Bois's message of achieving civil rights sooner rather than later.

CHAPTER TEN

ALONZO HERNDON

Alonzo Herndon was born into slavery on a farm 40 miles (64.4 km) outside of Atlanta. He moved to Jonesboro in his early 20s and learned how to be a barber. Then Herndon moved to Atlanta, where he started working at a barbershop. Before long, Herndon owned three barbershops that offered services to wealthy whites. In 1905, he entered the insurance business. He helped make the Atlanta Mutual Insurance Association one of the most successful insurance companies in the South.

Herndon was a leader in the African American community and experienced the effects of racial tension firsthand. Through hard work, he eventually became the richest black person in America. Many people compared his story to that of Booker T. Washington. Herndon also won the praise of W. E. B. Du Bois. This is surprising since Du Bois and Washington looked at the fight for equality in dramatically different ways.

In the early 1900s, Alonzo Herndon had a house built for his family in Atlanta, Georgia. It was mostly constructed by African American craftsmen.

CHAPTER ELEVEN

CONTINUING TENSION

At the beginning of World War I, tensions remained high in Georgia. An event in 1915 left another black mark on the state.

In 1913, a Jewish man named Leo Frank was accused of murdering a 13-year-old girl who worked at his factory. Even though there wasn't much evidence against him, Frank was found guilty and sentenced to death. Nearly two years later, the governor of Georgia changed Frank's sentence to life in prison.

Despite what many people believed at the time, later studies show that Frank was almost certainly innocent. His murder shows the level of fear and distrust many white Georgians held for people who were considered different.

Read For Profit—GEORGIAN WANT ADS—Use For Results

POLICE HAVE THE STRANGLER

AUSTRIA WILL MOVE ALONE ON MONTENEGRO

DETAILS OF BIG PONY CONTEST ANNOUNCED

VOLS SCORE IN FIRST; BRADY OPPOSES BECK

Late this afternoon, Chief of Detectives Lanford made this important statement to a Georgian reporter: "We have the strangler. In my opinion the crime lies between two men, the negro watchman, Newt Lee and Frank. We have eliminated John Gantt and Arthur Mullinax."

FRANK AND NEGRO ARE GIVEN "THIRD DEGREE"

A few months after this ruling, an angry mob broke Leo Frank out of jail. They drove him more than 100 miles (160.9 km) away and hanged him in Marietta, Georgia. This was considered one of the worst hate crimes of the early 20th century. That same year, the Ku Klux Klan, a white supremacist group, was reborn. Members held a secret meeting at the top of Stone Mountain near Atlanta.

CHAPTER TWELVE

GIRL SCOUTS AND VOTES FOR WOMEN

As the New South era came to an end, women from Georgia became more vocal and active in their communities. Juliette Gordon Low was a Savannah native. She established the Girl Scouts, which were based on the British Girl Guides. Low was influenced by the founder of the Boy Scouts.

Rebecca Latimer Felton was the wife of a Methodist minister who entered politics. Felton was never elected to office, but she worked to get women the right to vote. In 1922, the Georgia Senate chose her to fill Thomas E. Watson's U.S. Senate seat for a day after his death.

By the 1920s, Georgia was not that different from the way it was in 1877. Many Georgians still lived in poverty, and the state had yet to become an industrial powerhouse. Change was taking place, but it happened so gradually that people didn't always notice.

GLOSSARY

activist (AK-tih-vist) Someone who acts strongly in support of or against an issue.

boycott (BOY-kaht) To join with others in refusing to buy from or deal with a person, nation, or business.

disenfranchise (dis-ehn-FRAN-chyz) To keep a group from a legal right or privilege, especially the right to vote.

efficient (ih-FIH-shent) Capable of producing desired results without wasting materials, time, or energy.

entrepreneur (on-truh-pruh-NUR) A person who organizes and operates a business.

exposition (ek-spuh-ZIH-shun) A public display, similar to a fair, that shows art and industrial advances.

legislature (LEH-jis-lay-chur) A body of people that has the power to make or pass laws.

minstrel show (MIN-strel SHOH) An act in which a performer impersonates a black person, often using African American songs and jokes about African Americans.

progressive (pruh-GREH-sihv) Wanting to make changes in order to improve something.

sharecropping (SHER-krah-ping) A system in which people farm land they don't own and share the crops with the landowner.

tension (TEN-shun) A state in which people, groups, or countries disagree with and feel anger toward each other.

vocal (VOH-kul) Expressing oneself freely.

white supremacy (WYT suh-PREH-muh-see) The belief that white people are better than those of other groups.

INDEX

PRIMARY SOURCE LIST

Page 5
The New South, supplement to *Harper's Weekly*. February 12, 1887. Published in New York, NY.

Page 7
Henry Woodfin Grady. Photograph by C.W. Mater. ca. 1889. Atlanta, GA. Now kept in the Library of Congress Prints and Photographs Division, Washington, D.C.

Page 13
Thomas E. Watson. Photograph. January 8, 1904. Now kept in the New York Public Library Digital Collections.

WEBSITES

Due to the changing nature of Internet links, PowerKids Press has developed an online list of websites related to the subject of this book. This site is updated regularly. Please use this link to access the list: www.powerkidslinks.com/sog/nse